HORSES and the HUMAN SOUL

ALSO BY JUDITH BARRINGTON

Lifesaving: A Memoir

Writing the Memoir: From Truth to Art

History and Geography

Trying to Be an Honest Woman

HORSES AND THE HUMAN SOUL

Judith Barrington

Story Line Press ▪ 2004

Cover and text design by Marcia Barrentine

Cover art: "Spirit Horse," by Dame Elizabeth Frink, R.A. (1930 – 1993), private collection, used by permission of her son, Lin Jammet.

First American Edition, 2004

1 2 3 4 5 6 7 8 9

Printed in the United States on acid-free paper.

LIBRARY OF CONGRESS CATALOGING-IN-PUBLICATION DATA
Barrington, Judith.
    Horses and the human soul : poems / by Judith Barrington.
        p. cm.
        ISBN 1-58654-040-8
        I. Title.
    PS3552.A73647H67 2004
    811'.54--dc22

                                            2004000076

Story Line Press
Three Oaks Farm
PO Box 1240
Ashland, Oregon 97520
541.512.8793
www.storylinepress.com

for Ruth

ACKNOWLEDGMENTS

I WOULD LIKE TO thank the editors of the following publications in which many of these poems, sometimes in a different form, appeared: *The American Voice:* "The Dyke with No Name Thinks about Landscape" and "Oil"; *Americas Review:* "Four Reasons for Destroying a Spider's Web" and "The Dyke with No Name Thinks about God"; *Calyx:* "Passages"; *Calapooya Collage:* "Harvest" and "Oil"; *Clackamas Literary Review:* "Horses and the Human Soul," "My Father's Smile," and "Ineradicable"; *The Daily Telegraph Arvon International Poetry Competition Anthology 2000* (U.K.): "The Dyke with No Name Thinks about God"; *Fireweed:* "Body Language," "Havahart Mousetraps," "At Soapstone Creek," and "Black Beauty"; *From Here We Speak: An Anthology of Oregon Poetry:* "Beating the Dog"; *The G.S.U. Review:* "Rimas Dissolutas at Chacala Beach"; *The Kenyon Review:* "Four Reasons for Destroying a Spider's Web" and "Why Young Girls Like to Ride Bareback"; *Luna:* "The Nature of Memory" and "Kinds of Sleep"; *Manzanita Quarterly:* "The Day After: September 12, 2001"; *Mr. Cogito:* "Photograph, Scotland, Circa 1950"; *Northwest Review:* "Quinag"; *Poems and Plays:* "Crows" and "When Someone You Love Has Drowned"; *Poetry London* (U.K.): "Harvest," "Living without Horses," and "Crows"; *The Portland Review:* "Rimas Dissolutas at Chacala Beach" and "When Someone You Love Has Drowned"; *The Potomac Review:* "The Day After War Breaks Out"; *The Rialto* (U.K.): "The Nature of Memory"; *Scent of Cedars:* "Passages"; *The Sow's Ear:* "Timing" and "Great Tree Falling"; *The Texas Observer:* "I Am Choma: Do Not Feed Me"; *The Women's Review of Books:* "A True Dog Story," "Before I Am Born," and "Adolescence."

"Harvest" was the winner of the 1991 Portland Poetry Festival Contest judged by Robert McDowell and Lex Runciman. "The Dyke with No Name Thinks about Landscape" was the winner of the 1996 Dulwich (U.K.) Festival Poetry Contest, judged by Mimi Khalvati. "Horses and the Human Soul" was the winner of the 1998 Clackamas Literary Review Poetry Contest, judged by Vern Rutsala. "Quinag" was the winner of the Portland (U.K.) Poetry Contest. "Ineradicable" was the winner of the 2002 Clackamas Literary Review Poetry Contest, judged by Jeff Knorr. "Fibonacci" was the winner of the 2003 Looking Glass Bookstore National Poetry Month Contest, judged by Paulann Petersen.

My thanks to the Poultry Group—Shelley Davidow, Molly Gloss, Bette Husted, Caroline Le Guin, and Ursula K. Le Guin; to my sister Ruth for sending me the card with Elizabeth Frink's "Spirit Horse"; and to Kelly Allan for her careful copyediting.

I am grateful to the Oregon Institute of Literary Arts for a grant and for residencies at Cottages at Hedgebrook, Centrum, and The Tyrone Guthrie Centre, Ireland, which assisted in the writing of these poems.

CONTENTS

☃ THE POEM

It hides in my heart, waiting as if
in the small circle at the middle
of the labyrinth. I walk towards it

but the path turns away by a purple foxglove
and I must follow the windings that will
in the end lead me to the center.

It smells of cedars and honey'd skin,
cappuccino with grated chocolate,
the brine of its own body's betrayal.

Like a chestnut horse, it hides in shadow,
one white sock and the moist gleam of an eye
announcing its steady presence.

It has lodged in my heart like a stone in the shoe:
each time the great muscle contracts
I feel it rubbing the same tender spot;

there is no avoiding it — no limping or hopping,
no shaking it to a more comfortable place,
no stillness that can ease the bruise

except the stillness of a motionless heart.
It is the door behind which somebody stands
waiting to kiss and be kissed.

HARVEST

When you're young and out at night
searching for your lost pony
the black sky leans on your shoulders
like a rucksack full of sins.

Under invisible stars
you carry the burdens: gates left unlatched,
temper-tantrums that sent the pony
bucking away in his field

and all those times
you laughed at the farmer,
a dour man who watched the sky
as harvest approached —

watched the corn ripen while you
and your pony cut the corners
of those brittle fields, flattening
his bread and butter.

When you're young and out at night
calling for your black pony
through field after field of grain
an owl flings itself down from an oak

and you make vows.
If only you could find the pony
but remember too the vows
you make and remake on a dark night, searching.

♘ QUINAG

Against the sky, jagged as a broken eggshell,
the peaks of Quinag loomed over boggy moors
where shadows skimmed the bowed heads of harebells
and bracken creaked like a barn door.

I was six that year and my mother was sad.
The laird in his kilt said, "Don't go up there alone."
"Bears still live in those caves," he said
and showed me a long, grey, bear bone.

On Loch Awe I rowed the boat through misty sky,
my father casting where the sea trout fed.
When the dog grabbed the leader and swallowed a fly,
he worked the barb from her throat and staunched the blood.

My sister kept chanting a brand new word: *sinister*
hissing it softly between her teeth: *sinister*
sliding it smoothly over rocks: *sinister* —
arched caves up there in the devil's cloister

where bones and bear teeth rattled their evil laugh.
On the peat by the burn we played hide and seek,
chanting to keep us safe the words we had found:
The sinister peaks of Quinag, oh the sinister peaks!

PHOTOGRAPH, SCOTLAND, CIRCA 1950

It's raining of course,
all contrast washed into grey
and more grey.
Grainy and flat:
insufficient light
in the lens of the cheap Kodak Brownie.

I stand small in huge wellingtons.
For once, my mother leans into me
as if to encircle
my six-year-old body
with her bulk.
Both our raincoats are like armor.

Somewhere inside the stiff gabardine
behind buckles and belts
under layers of wool and stretchy hidden things,
our skins' aroma of soap and longing
yields to the rubbery smell of mackintosh.
Our skins pretend they are strangers.

Surely it wasn't always like this
though I have no memory
of being held, no umbilical trace,
no aftertaste of that sudden milk.
How did my cheek learn to forget
the particular planes of that breast?

And what else of love and the body
was forgotten — even by that sixth year
on a dock in Scotland, my mother

sitting on a bollard, rope trailing
into the mist, insufficient light
on my upturned, hopeful face.

BLACK BEAUTY

For two years at least
Shirley Kipps and I were horses —
you could tell by the way we walked
tossing our manes and jangling our bits.

We trotted with our chins pulled in
then galloped aggressively
stomping the leading leg
till the soles of our feet hurt.

I was Black Beauty of course,
whinnying softly when the boy
(whom no one else could see)
came to me with a pocketful of sugar;

Shirley was Tiny —
sometimes a lowly carthorse,
sometimes even a donkey
kept as company for Black Beauty.

Sundays we would lope along the ridge,
clouds scudding, sea sparking,
and I would buck with joy
while Tiny trotted stiffly beside me

never arguing when I said
her red browband was tacky,
never threatening to kick or bite
until the day I made her pull a plough —

then she looked furious,
bared her yellow teeth
and galloped across the golf course
her shoes wreaking havoc with the tenth green.

Years later in Chinatown
I thought I saw Shirley
pulling a cartload of vegetables,
a little lame on the near side.

Her long ears drooped liked Tiny's
but when I turned to greet her
she twitched away a fly
and cut me dead.

♘ LIVING WITHOUT HORSES

I believe in the gift of the horse, which is magic…..
—*Maxine Kumin*

Living without horses
is like breathing into the lungs
but never further:
never deep into the great cavity below
where horses of emerald and blue
fill the void with their squeals,
their thudding feet,
their waltzes into deep space.

To live without horses
is to slow down on the Sunset Highway
at a glimpse of chestnut rump
or a pair of pricked ears
above a bay face with a kind eye
that gazes toward the forests
draped like shawls over the Coast Range
where bluejays and woodpeckers ring out false alarms

and to breathe in the sweat and dust
of the police horse found unexpectedly
tethered to your parking meter after lunch —
then, at night, to rewind the videotape over
and over as the Budweiser commercial
sends you flying with the royal herd,
manes and tails like curtains of water,
nostrils more finely flared than the shelled human ear,

their elephantine feet
pounding the doors of a shuddering underworld

in the slowest waltz you've ever heard —
until, suddenly
you're hearing it in your abdomen
and it spills over into arteries and bones
pulsing through all your crevices
like blood from the heart's pump.

To live without horses is to carry them with you always:
the one who lifted you over the tiger trap,
the one who kicked you when you deserved it,
and the dappled grey one who lay down under you
and died as you ran away
unable to stay with him on that path
beside the golf course, breathing in
what you would search and search for in the years to come.

☙ ADOLESCENCE

Oh that fox trot! How elusive the glide —
nothing trot-like about it: no
up-and-down *clip clop*, no staccato
neat, feet-on-the-beat, but rather

a slippery ooze across the floor, sweaty
hand on bare back, chin thrust
unctuously forward, torsos mashed
in the posture of rapid creep —

a Monty Python funny walk,
soles feeling their way down inch by inch
till boys' toes and girls' heels lightly kiss the boards —
the sudden synchronized jog — and back to the glide.

> I never got it. It was too brazen
> and apologetic at the same time. Or maybe
> I didn't understand the sex yet.

At fourteen it was beyond me — that parody
of the silent approach; I knew nothing of
the dramatic pause full of awful promise
whirling into the skirt-lifting spin —

nothing of the desire to fall backwards
hair cascading to the floor, or to step astride
a yielding body and support the curve of its spine
breasts thrusting up, right there in your face.

What I knew was the real trot — not foxy
but equine — as I rose in the stirrups
my back straight, black velvet hat
low on my eyebrows, innocent leather whip

careless across my right thigh.
What I knew was saddle and flank,
the trot that was blessedly one thing at a time —
as rhythmic as the clock that marked the passing of the teens.

> You could hear them coming.
> And then you could hear them going away.

♘ DAWN, SHOW DAY, 1955

　　Left over right; right over left —
his mane is so wiry it slices the cracks of my fingers.
　　Left over right; right over left —
he points one hind toe and juts out his hip while I braid:
　　three bands of black hair, right over left;
pull them tight to the center and hold with my thumb.
　　He blows out his breath, long eyelashes droop,
the sky in the east is gleaming, he closes his eyes.
　　Left over right; he twitches his neck
at a fly, he is dreaming, the fly keeps on touching his ears.
　　He is dreaming of Ireland (right over left)
of the stone wall, his mother's rough tongue, and milk in his mouth.
　　The fly's on his forehead; he dreams of a ship
where the floor slips away, his mother is gone, and the world
　　is tilting below him, left over right,
while the haynet sways. The fly's on his eye as I roll
　　the small braid and sew it with needle and thread.
The sun casts a ray at the fly — its marvelous blue
　　all polished and perfect and, left over right,
I begin on another, he switches hind legs, and his dream
　　tastes of clover; the fly's gone; right over left.

The thing that makes me crazy is
how much I wanted her —
the simple act of longing
year after year, till finally
she took my hand and held it
pressed to her small right breast.
That kind of longing
turns your whole torso into a cavern
where despair echoes wall to wall
and hope leaps like a foetus.
My complicity confuses the issue.
How to say the word: abuse
when my body tells another story —
not a tale of clenched self-protection
but an epic, my young arm
reaching out for her breast,
my back spreading wide to her touch?

The thing I go back to is
the rain on the window —
water washing all over the pane
as hand moves to breast
and someone seduces someone else.
My complicity clouds the definitions
like that misted window,
one side of its thin old glass
steaming with the heat of breath and skin
while the other
leans into the storm, weeping.

THE NATURE OF MEMORY

for Colin

Not remembering
where I slept the night before the wedding
where I put on the dress (white, brocade)
or who, if anyone, helped me.
Not remembering where the car picked me up
and my brother in the car with me:
what did he say then?

Remembering two large brandies
and the metallic taste on the way to the church
but, after that, only what's recorded
in pictures or the silver-printed program
and that's not real remembering.
The group on the grass and the wind;
my hair so stiff with lacquer it leans all in a block
instead of blowing strand by strand across my face.
Your mother holding her hat on
caught by the camera for ever and ever amen,
and now she's dead holding her hat on.

Remembering my largeness in the dress (white, brocade)
your neatness in the morning suit
and the ginger of your sideburns.
Remembering the bones that whispered no
the pain as I smiled
the silence as I spoke
and the cold as I blushed warm and held your willing arm.

Not remembering my yes.

THE DYKE WITH NO NAME THINKS ABOUT GOD

Long ago in Spain, she watched women climb the steps to
the huge basilica across the square, scarves tied over their hair,
heads down as they sidled in, furtive in their great desire.

She envied their passion — the soaring vault under which they knelt,
the gaunt body of the statue whose eyes rolled up white and resigned
from the head that lolled to one side, resting on ribs,

the banks of candles sputtering in holy air,
and the great lover waiting back there in the darkness.
The dyke with no name recognized the secret thrill

masked by downcast eyes and the fear of discovery
when they glanced across the square towards her window
as if they felt her watching. But what she recognized most

as they slid through the enormous brass-studded door,
was their shame — the way their bodies shrank into the black
folds of their clothes as if to say *I'm sorry,* as if to say

I'm full of unseemly passions, as if to say, as she herself would say
through the years to come: *I am unworthy; I am nothing;*
and, in the seductive light of a thousand candles: *I am yours.*

WHY YOUNG GIRLS LIKE TO RIDE BAREBACK

You grasp a clump of mane in your left hand,
spring up and fall across her back;
then, pulling on the wiry black hair
which cuts into your palm and fourth finger,
haul yourself up till your right leg
swings across the plump cheek of her hindquarters.

Now you hold her, warm and alive, between your thighs.
In summer, wearing shorts, you feel the dander
of her coat, glossy and dusty at the same time,
greasing up the insides of your calves,
and as she walks, each of your knees in turn
feels the muscle bulge out behind her shoulder.

Trotting's a matter of balance. You bounce around
unable to enter her motion as you will when the trot
breaks and she finally waltzes from two to three time.
Nothing to be done at the trot but grab again that mane
that feels, though you don't yet know it, like pubic hair,
and straddle her jolting spine with your seat bones

knowing that when the canter comes, you will suddenly
merge — you and that great, that powerful friend:
she, bunching up behind, rocking across the fulcrum,
exploding forward on to the leading leg, and you
digging your seat down into the sway of her back,
your whole body singing: *we are one, we are one, we are one.*

THE DYKE WITH NO NAME THINKS ABOUT LANDSCAPE

1

At first it wasn't landscape at all.
Where you live is just where you live:

a place to walk about in,
drive your car through on the way to somewhere,

notice on a pretty day
when clouds are puffs and grasses blowing just so.

From a horse's back, tracking the skyline
grey sea became grey sky

and chalky paths down the escarpment
gashed the smooth flank of the downs.

Leaning over to unhook the chain
of a five-bar gate, she knew

just how fast to sidle the horse through
before the metal gate swung back with a clang

and the horse twitched an ear —
too familiar with the sound to make a fuss.

The windmills, Jack and Jill, spread their sails
and grew as organic as gorse bushes

or hares on the barren plough
but their spread sails remained unmoved

by the great wind which stirred up a great wave
in the grasses from Firle to Beachy Head.

Up there on her horse she too grew
organic as winter wheat

never naming the villages far below:
Poynings, Ditchling, Fulking, Steyning

distant clusters of roofs that revealed to her,
as if through a telescope,

a particular lytch gate, a brick well,
a post office serving cream teas.

2

When she left it became landscape —
a beloved green painting hauled around in her mind

while the next one (ochre and sage) unfolded
smelling of Mediterranean pine in the afternoon

and the one after that (sepia and umber)
threw open its chest and sang.

In these landscapes too, she wanted to grow organic —
spreading her limbs to the sky

on that almost-flat rock that jutted from the river
and held her between two swirling streams.

Pinpoints of spray pricked her skin
which dried and dried between the divided waters

while the river too — turbulence, rocks,
moss, trout, and human body —

pried open the hot thighs of the desert
with the persuasive pressure of wetness.

Was it then that it started —
then she began to feel the eyes watching?

In each landscape, people grew from the shadows.
In each landscape, people belonged.

But here on her rock,
head in the *V* of the parted waters

the dyke with no name sees herself
as if with eyes watching from the hill above,

sees the desert intersected by river,
sees ponderous rocks, shaggy falls, the cruising hawk,

and herself, a human figure growing from shadows,
herself in the frame, on the rock, not belonging.

3

The trouble is not nature, she thinks,
but the people who tell you there's always one of each —

starting with Noah
and his couple-filled floating zoo.

Pistils and stamens, winged seeds from trees,
insects waving their various appendages:

she remembers her smudgy drawings from biology;
she knows what they left out and why.

The trouble with pastoral scenes is the lovers —
the hand-in-hand, one-of-each, lover and his lass.

She knows it's more than looking wrong in the picture.
But does she know it's a matter of life and death?

4

Whose life? Whose death?
All she wanted was to move again like the winter wheat

to live in her skin touching the earth's skin
to feel spray and rock and the finger of the sun.

Once, a long time ago, she made love
on a hilltop under copper beech trees:

leaves turned to mulch underneath her
as she breathed the sky through her lover's hair

and somewhere close by a pony snickered —
a friendly snicker; an acknowledgment.

She still remembers what it felt like to lie in those arms:
some of them beech roots, others human and female,

trusting the pony like a brother,
the sky looking down the same way she looked up.

That was before the two hikers were shot —
the two women, stalked for days by the man

who killed one and left the other for dead.
One each for life and death as it turned out.

5

There is nothing organic about cars.
They skim across surfaces, separated

from the landscape by hard, black tarmac:
no danger of putting down roots.

Even when a car disintegrates in the ground,
blackberries filling the bent frame of its windshield,

rusty chassis sinking into the earth
to blue up some passing hydrangea,

even then, its chrome and oil and plastic seats
spurn the comfort of ordinary rot.

The dyke with no name kept moving,
her rubber tires grabbing the blacktop with a squeal

as she pushed sideways through bends,
kept everything skidding.

Tall haystacks with poles poking out the top
dashed by her window. She noted their shape,

their resemblance to some señorita's hair
held up by a protruding pin.

She watched the show through glass
as if she had put in her penny on the pier,

watched herself from the hillside above
speeding through picture after picture

silk headscarf flying, arm on the door tanned
hands turning the small leather wheel.

Sometimes, when her head raged with pain
she parked the car in a field and slept,

all doors locked, all windows up
while the grasses tickled the hot skin of her tires.

6

Now she is lying on a blanket, the sand below
moulded to the shape of her body.

Sudden swells slap the shore beyond her feet:
a barge has passed by,

trudging down river with its load
like a good-natured shire horse

its throbbing lost now behind the breaking
of that great wave which seems to rise from the deeps.

The turbulence is quick: a lashing of the sand
followed by September's lazy calm

as the river moves unseen again,
cows from another world low on the far shore

and the seagull's body, a fragile handful,
dangles gently between its two tremendous wings.

The trouble is not nature, she thinks
but the people who say I'm not part of it.

They're trying to paint me out of the landscape
says the dyke with no name

but her thighs in hot sand remember a horse's warm back
as the wind makes a great wave from Oregon to Beachy Head.

RIMAS DISSOLUTAS AT CHACALA BEACH

> *… not waving but drowning.*
> *—Stevie Smith*

Not even your hand reaching from the past as you go down
into the Atlantic keeps me from the sea. Pacific waves like trucks
crash down on me, my legs tugged away in an avalanche of sand.
Sometimes I fall, suck in a snatch of salty air
and skid into the cave of the next wave, only to be hauled
back to the tideline with bottle caps, shells and small green beads.

With an arm raised, that visual cliché, is not how you went down
I'm sure — it's how *we* went down in the pool at Black Rock:
leggy ten-year-olds each holding her nose with one hand
and reaching up with the other in that mocking gesture of despair.
Down we went, face to face, our hair loosing small
bubbles as it streamed upwards and we stared like mermaids

into that liquid underworld, clear and paint blue, its only known
danger a dose of chlorine that left us headachy and pink-
eyed, our swimsuits smelling of hospital by the long day's end.
Did we sense then, as our lungs screamed for air
and our cheeks bulged with held breath, that this transparent wall
could surge into the hollows of our lungs and turn us to weed?

The fact is that after a while I couldn't stop. Rhythmically, alone,
I surged up, grabbed a mouthful of air and sank,
my arm marking the spot in a drama that would never end.
As it turned out, it was a kind of defiance of the future
as it is now of the past when I breast the Pacific, ignoring the call
of your hand in the air as Atlantic swells cover your head.

the sky over the sea is a piece of Turner's art,
but inland, over the mountains, a gull's-back sky
speaks of soft weather while cows in soggy fields
wait for the milking dusk. Out west
beyond the beach, surf flies from a dark wall
of water you can hardly bear to look at —
so easily could it suck and swallow you up.
Then it is you know that you are nothing.

At low tide, when black clouds slide apart,
breakers far out on the sandbanks tumefy.
In spite of yourself you watch them build
until one emerges like a royal beast
with foaming crown and begins to roll
towards you — a muscular horse with his matted
wind-thrashed mane shedding barnacles and scup.
You are not surprised. Now you are sure you are nothing.

Sometimes, even by a lake in summer's heat,
you sit on a rock in crisp bracken, dry
and warm, while the hawk stalks a likely kill.
Water blows toward you, furrowing fast
into tiny waves that slap ferns and boulders
with muffled splashes. When someone you looked at
with love has drowned, even a ripple can rise up
like a mountain until you know you are sinking.

You stay there on your rock, or your beach, and wait
while the wave bears down, lifts higher and higher,
begins to froth and lick its briny lips. Still
you grow smaller, the sky grows vaster,

and under the wave's rim, arms and legs fall
like sticks and the Os of drowned mouths spit
pebbles. At last the wave dies, pooling in your footsteps.
You turn to the east where cows are patiently waiting.

♻ MY FATHER'S SMILE

It is that hour of the night when most people die.
Outside, close by, the tallest branches of hawthorn,
new-leafed, bow and duck as the wind torments them,
        eases up, and flees.

Once I saw Plath's yew tree pose grandiose
against her howling Devonshire sky, but here
there is no moon and the hawthorn, etched on a yellowish
        night, portends nothing

except perhaps the first bird call — coming now
as some small sparrow feels the approaching dawn.
Light, she knows, will creep this way from Idaho,
        touching the slopes of mountains,

and dragging along that daily dose of hope
that enters our bones for minutes or hours, depending
upon the day. Likely as not, I'll forget
        again to be grateful — forget

to greet all those who arrive: my mother, her knees
spread wide like Gertrude Stein's, my father forever
jingling the change in his pocket, a smile on his face
        that I finally understand.

Phones will begin to ring as the sky grows grey
and a bluejay, unnoticed by all but the cat in the window,
will come in to land on the hawthorn. The dead will dance
        all day on those new leaves

among the thorns that will tear your hands if you touch.
All day I will carry my father's smile on my face
to keep me from seeing them out there, cold in the wind,
    I'll smile, not letting them in.

♄ HAVAHART MOUSETRAPS

"The humane mousetrap: trap and release!"

The very first day
one of the doors had sprung shut.
I held the trap gingerly —
thought I felt the weight
of the small body
as we headed for the cemetery,
me and the dog,
to liberate the captive.
("The far end of the cemetery"
you said as I left.)

By a sturdy oak
I assumed the mouse-release position:
feet apart, the little coffin
that was not a coffin
pointed like a garden hose.
The mouse, I knew, would leap
in a graceful arc
and the dead would laugh
at this small resurrection
in their midst.

But what of the two mourners
at the grave down the way —
one kneeling now to place
flowers in a jar beside the stone —
what would they think
as I stood pointing my box
at the falling leaves

playing god, here
where god had played
a different game with them?

Perhaps they thought
I was practising tai chi
as I leaned slowly forward,
and brought my left hand up
to release the door.
Did they know I was holding a body? —
not for burial like theirs
but for simpler return to the earth:
not a quickening, not a miracle,
just a sudden scurry into dry leaves.

There is the sleep of the black boots
standing, pigeon-toed, in the closet,
exhausted from all that purposeful striding.

There is the sleep of the red silk tie,
looped like a dead snake over the hook
no longer knotted and butch.

There is the sleep of the moon
above her threadbare mat of cloud,
her half-open eye glinting at my nakedness,

and there is the swift, sleepless river which dreams
and dreams for the women who hold each other
on its bank, not yet dreaming for themselves.

♺ TIMING

for Amy Clampitt

The horse and I, as one, observe the fence ahead,
check our speed till we are cantering almost on the spot,
all the while measuring, with our common eye, the distance
back to where we are now from the takeoff point.
Muscles and blood both know that the takeoff point
is as far in front of the fence as the fence is high.

The mare quivers, gathers her weight over hind legs,
waiting for me to agree with her on the place
where we will let go — the place from which
three enormous strides will take us to that spot.
If we get it right, we'll simply stride on into air,
arcing as if through the sky and over the moon.

I'd like to believe it's all in the preparation:
one, two, three: SOAR! my riding instructor shouted
and I'd hear it years later in the green Triumph,
as I measured the approach to each tight bend,
headlights grabbing the gleaming cats' eyes:
the flexible spine of the narrow Welsh road.

Off to my right, a river dashed over rocks
as I eased my foot off the gas and waited for the moment
to turn the wheel, grip the whole car in my hands,
and accelerate through the curve with a graceful drift.
The brick walls of the bridge trapped crisp exhaust,
then hurled the sound straight up toward the stars.

49

This question of timing, though, has its limitations:
what of the fence you can't see, a looming catastrophe
as you round the bend? — no time to count your paces;
no time for the little dance that leads to grace.
And what of the curve just over the brow of the hill
that ducks away to the left under airborne wheels?

If it weren't for such things, would I die in my bed at ninety —
letters and receipts stacked under amber paperweights,
library books returned, wisdom dispensed
to great-nieces? — Would I time it just right to the end,
plan my approach and measure my strides to the edge?
Getting it right, would I soar into indigo air?

BEATING THE DOG

She lowered her belly into heather
and froze. Her nose explored
the breeze, sorted smells of weather
from what mattered. I saw how her eyes stared.

She was so young then, downwind
from two sheep on a hillside purple under blue;
there were farmers with guns in my mind
as I yelled NO. I was young too.

It was no use my yelling.
The sheep lifted their heads too high
and bolted, swerving, almost falling
over tussocks, while the sky

tilted and spun as I ran,
the dog ran, we barked and yelled
and the four of us alone up there
ploughed through bracken and harebells.

She heard me at last, left
the sheep heaving and bleating
by a gorse bush. Her eyes softened,
she crouched, and then I was beating

the dog with the leash,
farmers and guns in my mind
as rage washed over the hill
like a storm's hot wind.

I remember how she screamed twice
before I sank down in the heather.
It doesn't matter that she licked my face —
the sorry tears; it doesn't matter

that she barked and skipped through the stream
or that she never stared that way
at a sheep again. Ends and means.
How could things be simple after that day?

When Bradshaw's master listed him
in the telephone directory
the humans found it funny.
But Bradshaw went on hunting rats
in the barn, cheerful in his
brown and white terrier outfit.

Soon he had his choice of outfits
as catalogs from gentlemen's tailors
thumped through the mailslot:
"Brady Marsh Esquire," they said
on personalized address labels, but Bradshaw
gripped them in his teeth and shook hard.

The humans laughed themselves silly
when someone called wanting his opinion:
What was his favorite TV show?
What brand of toothpaste did he use?
"Brady can't come to the phone," they said,
"He's out in the grain bins chasing a rat."

They sent him Dutch bulb catalogs,
coupons for free pizzas,
and once even a special dog food offer
but it wasn't a brand he liked
so he took the coupon instead and buried it
with some rabbit bones behind the shed.

"Play dead, Bradshaw," ordered the humans
as he rolled on his wide little back.
But when he got old, he refused
the trick and spent more time in the barn
dozing with the horses. He ignored his mail
with its ads for the finest funerals.

THE POWER OF THINGS

for Paul Merchant, William Stafford Archivist

Boxes lined up in file cabinets;
dated sheets with angular writing in dark ink —
the morning habit of the poet, a dream
traveling through dark to merge with waking thought,
a poem snapping at its heels:
the little daily dog eager to be let out.

Seeing his pages there is like sitting at that grave
twenty years ago — square block rising from long grass
where we leaned our backs against the writer's name
her long-ago *Vindication* suddenly the work of a woman,
pen in hand, ink in well, long skirt brushing
the enduring weeds with their purple flowers.

I knew their work, these two artisans of justice
and the word. I knew their habits — his couch-dreaming
at dawn, her startling call for a little fairness — but
it's things that make the knowing different:
small knobs in the tombstone pressing into my back,
the slashing line through a wrong word on his page

and, for a moment, outside the archives' window
or in that lush graveyard, a burst of birdsong
followed by a quietness through which I discern
the regular breathing of someone nearby.

1 Wood Becomes Paper Becomes Word

The crack is sharp like a pistol shot.
It rings out above the messy noise of chainsaws
and debris falling into itself.
One by one their backs break, each one a scream.

The poet sits all day beside the creek.
She cannot see the hill, three-quarters bald
and littered with limbs. But she hears the trucks leave
each bearing three royal bodies tied down with wire.

Bones are cracking all around in the air:
birdlike bones of the child whose feet must be bound;
strong bones forced backwards in a prison cell.
What words can come from this? What words must come?

2 You There…

Put the palms of your hands together
close to your body, thumbs touching your chest
then bow your head to the tree
whose body bears these words.

In the deep pool under the cedar
a trout rises to a mayfly and ripples spread
in widening Os like the years
etched into heartwood as it grows.

What have the years written into your body?
What patterns emerged as you passed through fire?

Put your palms together, lifeline to lifeline.
Bow your head for the history you bear.

3 Blood

My blood came late. No one celebrated
when I passed through the gate and emerged
hardly ready to be woman. Blood spoke then as it did later,
refusing to flow when I denied the first great grief.

No tears. No blood. Body a dry creekbed,
the mouth of everything parched.
When the blood returned I didn't know
how to welcome it, or even that I should.

No one told me to paint it onto parchment —
to make the great red swirls into horses
or dance it into an offering, hot as the fire
which finally scorched my heart.

Blood is leaving now and I will celebrate.
Along the creekbed, the gravel where salmon spawn
and the smooth black rocks beside the stream
will bear many footprints, fading red.

4 Stories

Her hand lies against white pine board,
the lines of her palm, some say, telling her life story.
White pine has a story too, etched into grain,
and she listens hard for that whispered tale
ignored by loggers on the hardtack hill
and the man at the lumberyard, slapping down planks.

A deep hum of silence surrounds hand and wood —
the silence of a garden walled from the city
where a child once pressed her body into wet earth
while trees moved their shadows across her,
the greens all around turned dark,
and small snails, with their spiral shells, whistled shanties.

Footprints in wet earth become footprints in pine;
the journey of a tree and its body
translated by the sculptor and her tools.
Inside the wood are dead birds from the garden
and the trails of ants never forgotten.
Inside the wood is a forest. A mother. A ship.

5 Feet

In my family we all have them — these feet
with the toes pulled back and curled under,
holding on for dear life. In the hospital now
my brother, threaded like a huge bead
onto tubes that enter and leave his body,
tugs at his oxygen mask and sleeps to the beep of machines.

We walk from one age to another,
at first discarding the past, striding eagerly
into double figures, not looking for heartbreak,
but later learning to hold on with hands and feet
to what went before, wary now of each new doorway
until the heart, too, learns to hang back.

In the east they say that the whole body
is mapped on our feet. The heart is there,
crouched between tendon and bone: rub that spot

and the heart will be brave. My brother curls
and uncurls his toes unsure whether to let go or hold fast.
Which door does he face now? Who will hold his cold feet?

6 What We Say

We say the tree is dead
    when leaves curl and crisp, spotted yellow
    or needles turn brown and fall to the ground
    leaving their branches naked.
We say the tree is dead
    when the trunk loses its sap
    and one bare spar points to the sky
    pocked deep with the work of the woodpecker.
We say the tree is dead now
    when it falls like thunder
    tearing limbs from adjacent maples
    to stretch out its huge body on the earth.
Yes, we say, the tree is really dead
    as it softens there on the humus
    and saplings emerge from its hip, its barrel chest,
    well nursed as they talk back and grow leggy.
When is the tree ever dead? I say. Table? Beam?
    Window frame seen and touched, holding and held?
    We say we, too, are dead when breath and blood
    no longer rise, and limbs fail to move in the wind.
Lightning brings fire; burial slow rot,
    but scattered ashes are breathed in by strangers,
    graves visited, talked to, peed on by dogs —
    and stories are told of holding and being held.

AT SOAPSTONE CREEK

in memoriam: Will Martin

His ashes fertilize these familiar trees,
random roots sucking him up
till he is given away to the mist,
needles and leaves exhaling his name.

Though I never knew him, I see him
hammering these fine light planks,
the stairs that rise and rise to his study
way above the creek, his dream
of a child's treehouse made manifest
through long days of sawing.

At night, by glow of the oil lamps,
he played dominoes with his dad,
their scores recorded in the black-bound journal
beside watercolors of bugs like gems,
pencil plans for the covered bridge
and the musings of his last descending mood.

What does it mean, anyway, to know someone?
There's talk and touch, yes;
there's light on the brightness of hair
and a catch of breath close by in the night.
But there's this knowing too: the music of his chosen creek;
the yellow sheen on wood he worked with his hands.

↻ WALKING NORTH

for Nancy

Think of your life as a beach —
a wide, smooth-sanded Oregon beach,
the sea on your left as you walk north
and on your right a range of dunes
changing outlines from year to year.

Sometimes the sand gleams with mica;
waves slip up leaving a scalloped border
where you tread softly with bare feet.
Sometimes days crash in on you,
spittle from the surf flying in your face,
your boots leaving a trail of small ponds.

But always as you head for the mist-hung
headland you will reach one day — always
there's that single set of footprints ahead.
You recognize those prints: your mother made them
long ago when she walked through the years
you've come to know — thirty-five, forty-eight —
always stepping in the faint shadows of her feet.

And then they're gone. Sand stretches away
unmarked except by wind and gulls' feet:
you are as old as your mother was when she took
her final step. For a moment you wonder can you go on?
Icy wind snatches at your scarf and you stagger,
footprints weaving among a thousand small shells.

Think of your life as a beach you can walk alone
even when mist comes down and you know you are lost.
Walking north, the cold may burn your cheeks.
But when you rest, dunes will hold you on their breasts
and two boys will be walking in the prints you left behind.

♌ OIL

Oars dip and pull.
Blades lift, soundlessly dripping oil
into the slick sea.
Oarlocks squeak
and mist shrouds the rowboat
where we huddle inside our coats.
Somewhere in these shallows
birds are dying.

Oars dip again
and the mist opens for us.
When I look back
it has closed
like the net curtain let fall
across a neighbor's window.
Someone is watching
what we do here.

My neck hurts
as it used to
after the long drive to Wales
through dark and rain
my chin poked forward
owls haunting the edge of vision.
If I had a wing
I'd put my head under it.

And if I had two wings
I'd need them to fan out —
the feathers crisp
beads of water rolling off like tears

the bones spread
like fingers over my face.
I'd need this water to be clean
when my body paused midair and lightly dropped.

↻ WE

after Mahmoud Darwish

We walk on paths of pine needles between trilliums fading to
    purple.
We sing as we walk, even in the rain.
We do not know about the man with the gun always behind,
    always out of sight.
We climb into a pickup truck with strangers who smile before they
    tie us to a gate and set about us with tire irons.
In the park, sometimes, but not always, we avoid the shadows.
In the street by the docks, sometimes we refuse to keep our
    distance from one another.
In the forest, we listen to the warnings of bluejays and hold hands.

We harvest the murdered boy from the fencepost where his body
    hangs, bloody and limp.
His mother says, "Matthew was a fine boy."
We watch the other mothers on television — the one whose son was
    dragged behind a Chevy till his head was severed.
We harvest what we can from the fields which are flooded with
    briny water.
Under the moon, fenceposts cast long shadows and strands of wire
    seem beautiful.
We walk under stars that change the color of our hair.
Stones gleam in the stubble left by the scythe.

I AM CHOMA: DO NOT FEED ME

*Sign on the monkey's cage at the Hotel
Molino de Agua, Puerto Vallarta*

A small girl-child, human,
strokes the cloud-grey fur
of my long arm, stretched out
under the netting. Outside.

In the shadows, my arm lies in dust,
angled at the joints,
built to swing my small body
in the cheerful company of my clan

along complex high-forest paths —
to grasp each branch between thumb and fingers,
rotate with the arc of my momentum, and let go:
catch and fly, catch and fly, catch and fly.

In the well of deep shadow under the mango tree
the girl-child touches me
and my one touched limb lies
quietly beside her. Outside the cage.

She touches in the rhythm of repeated hellos
her fingers in my fur saying *I'm sorry.*
Her fingers, parting my fur carefully
saying *I'm here with you now.*

HORSES AND THE HUMAN SOUL

Undercover investigators in Tallahassee, Florida watched two men break a thoroughbred's right rear leg with a crowbar at 10:10 p.m. The men were part of a nationwide ring that injured horses to collect on insurance policies.
—The Oregonian

1

The bay mare lifts her head and listens.
There is darkness, the new moon barely revealing
trunks of scrub oak beside her meadow.

A car door has slammed.
The mare shifts her hoofs in the wet grass,
her belly round with the sweet spring growth.

Frogs are merely a backdrop of sound —
as much part of her world
as the post and rail fence against which

she scratches her rump
or the stamp stamp of Bess and William in the afternoon
when the sun is up and the flies biting.

A figure steps from the oaks, metal scoop in his hand.
He holds it out, jiggles it
till the mare hears the familiar sound of sifting oats.

2

They say when you dream a horse
that horse is your spirit.

Once the horse I dreamed
looked out of a trailer pulled by an old Volvo,

the driver a woman who one day
would teach me something about the spirit.

She drove carefully.
The horse was safe.

When you dream a horse it had better be safe
or we are all in trouble.

3

Did the investigators hide behind those same scrub oaks? Did they
wear grey suits and carry notebooks as they pushed their way
through the lush undergrowth? Did their ball point pens carry the
name of their company? Did they smoke as they waited for the
sound of the car or did they talk about money or football or the
girls in the office? Did it occur to them then, as the man led the
mare back to his friend with the crowbar, that they could stop this
before it happened? Did the new moon shed enough light for them
to see as the crowbar hit the right rear leg just below the hock, the
blood spurted, the rich brown hair mixed with splintered bone, and
the mare screamed, or did they have to note which leg it was later,
after the arrest? And what happened to their souls? What hap-
pened to them? I want to know that.

CROWS

Crows startle the clouds
with grievances never resolved
and warnings blurted into thin air.

Once in a while, the cries of all those who tried to survive
pour from the funnels of their throats.
No wonder we never really listen.

Like most animals, crows tell the truth:
working hard to penetrate our tiny tubular ears,
they cackle on telephone lines while we watch TV.

Once I did listen to a crow, but even when I had heard
his whole story, there was nothing I could do.
Next, I thought, I'd have to listen to squirrels and coyotes.

I like to think I deal with my share of rotten truths
but I couldn't bear to kneel down in damp grass
and listen to the hedgehog or the mole.

♻ SUICIDE PACT

The war is like a desperate illness.
                                    —*Virginia Woolf*

The hospital train: *grieving & tender*
& heavy laden carries the wounded
across a viaduct, high above hedgerows,
brick arches vaulting to the sky.
Below, uneasy sheep wait for a plane
to skim the treetops and set them off again:
stampede! — huge fleeces wagging — scatter! scatter!
They won't know which way to run and many will fall
to lie on their backs till their hearts explode
and their eyeballs roll back. Yes, this is terror.

Morphia in my pocket, writes the novelist
and hurries across the downs to look at the wreck —
a friendly one, crashed at Southease,
the usual hum of flies in the air
and the mutter of afternoon village life.
Leonard, her Jewish husband, waiting for tea
has morphia too in case the Germans should land.
I'll walk and ride these same downs for years,
not seeing the bomb craters under the wheat,
Roman forts embracing the graves of planes.

♅ BEFORE I AM BORN

Raids over Brighton this afternoon —
the Germans grumbling in, squeezing out bombs

and my mother hurries at the sound of the siren,
wooden pegs marking her trail from clothesline to house

as if she might need them later — after the all-clear
to find her way back to the basket of sodden socks:

not bread crumbs in a forest nor twine in a maze
but the careless scatter of someone interrupted at work.

She's used to it now but still she's inclined to panic
when she heads for the cellar, hoping her children are safe

in the shelter at school; it's more like a game to them —
my brother and sister at war before I am born

delighted to leave their history or algebra class
and descend to the musty space where children kick feet

and pass round illegal toffees from fist to fist
while a teacher's eyes scan the ceiling as if to watch

for the barrels of death as they somersault out of the sky.
My father, headed home on an early train

hears the defending planes above the rattle
of wheels that slow and speed up as if to dodge

the dogfight unfolding above the flank of the downs.
Hornets swarmed over my head the novelist notes

while father returns to his paper then dozes and smokes.
Sheep frightened, I'll read in the diary years later

and imagine them there — their fleeces swaying,
their rotten hoofs giving way as they stumble downhill.

INERADICABLE

Sigmund Gundle, 1915 – 1996

He'll never forget their names: daughter
granddaughter, sister, late wife.
He'll always know where he parked the car
and what he went to the store for in the first place.

The President's name, today's date, his favorite
brand of coffee — all etched
like the names of the dead in a granite wall,
alphabetical. Memory's like that, isn't it? —

dark grey wall, file cabinet, a great room
with newspapers piled in rows by date and place
all of them recording news of a life
from gossip column to missile attack to the daily puzzle.

Or, of course, it's a computer: cerebral megabytes
swallow the story chapter by chapter
until the hard drive crashes….
What he thought could never be lost, *is* lost:

names escape through paneless windows,
streets sprout unexpected turns
and faces float away from their old histories.
He turns his wheelchair to block the corridor;

nurses beg him to move but he waves them away
shouting in German. So much is erased
but this he'll remember and remember:
the camp; the guards; yellow star; dead mother.

THE DAY AFTER WAR BREAKS OUT

Squirrels in the cemetery
are reckless, dashing around
as they do when the first grip of winter
brings home the sober news:
food may be short —
supplies in the wrong cache.

The afternoon is luminous
as if just in this one place
among the accumulated wisdom
of old and various trees
the air has gathered more than its share
of benevolent light.

In North America
in the first years of the century
I could go on recording
the wisdom of trees
the quality of light
and still call myself a poet —

but in the war zone the afternoon is luminous too:
the glow of burning bodies
trapped under a black ceiling
of North American smoke —
the white light seeping
from the eyeball of somebody's friend.

FOUR REASONS FOR DESTROYING A SPIDER'S WEB: A MEDITATION DURING THE GULF WAR

One: It is in your way,
strung across a doorway
or between the forest walls
flanking your trail.
It floats like a mantra
across the steps down from your deck
and you cannot duck under
or walk around the other way.
You've tried.
There is no secret password
at which, when you utter it,
one filament will let go
and the whole web swing back intact
closing silently behind you.

Two: You don't like spiders.
It's not a violent dislike —
just the kind that makes you shudder
when you feel the web caress your face.
Where is the spider? you wonder
as your smallest hairs prick up
and somewhere in your brain
a picture of that arachnoid body
dropping inside your shirt
opens like the iris of the camera's eye —
gone before the thought.
You try to be careful
as you break the web at one corner
and its tenant falls away, glaring.

Three: Spiders belong in the wild
and yours is human territory —
sterile, cleansed of everything that grows
outside your control.
You scrub lichen and moss from bathroom tiles,
smother the prolific earth with concrete,
and watch out for those beasts
that swim and swim through the plumbing.
Somewhere in your immaculate brain
you know a spider's web is a symbol —
not the great-grandmother spread across the sky
but wayward nature getting the better of you.
You keep a special broom for the ones slung,
gaudy with dew, between your sculptured shrubs.

Four: Killing things gives you a fix,
so you tear out the web
with one wild grab of your hand
and watch the small body plop down.
When it scuttles away, one step,
one foot grinding it to a pulp
and you smile. Something in your brain
gives a little, eases up.
Sometimes you speak to the body
flattened to a smear on the floor:
"Little bastard," you sneer
and the thing in your brain hums a sweet song.
Or "goddamn black fucker,"
as you grind your teeth and grin.

↻ ON DISCOVERING THAT LIFE IS NOT A MOVIE

We simulate disaster, first with models
then with computers that make buildings
burn and fall, bodies fly through air,
cars leap up and fall on their heads, blazing.

We create severed legs and heads sheared from bodies.
Ketchup is blood and blood becomes ketchup
until one day we see: *oh it is blood* —
life blood pouring from blue veins.

　　We do not simulate grief. Long, long grief.
　　Or psyches that leap into space, severed from hearts.

Stunt men fall forty floors, bounce and roll:
stand up; rub their chins; get paid; go home.
Actors lie down for the rape scene
while someone, somewhere, composes a suitable rape score.

Special effects bring the plane into line,
cut to the passengers' wide eyes,
cut to the hero, flying, flying, to catch them all in his one hand,
cut to the bodies falling. But where is the hand?

　　We do not simulate the long silence.
　　The soundtrack is unusually quiet.

THE DAY AFTER: SEPTEMBER 12, 2001

Molivos, Greece

First, through dreams, come the doves
hoo-hooing like soft owls.
Twice they call, then pause before the third question.
If I knew the answer, I would call back
but the notes just hang there, hundreds of them,
like ornaments swaying on the dawn tree.

Then the donkey begins his sad-funny bray:
squeaky whistle followed by the creak and groan
of some door in a Gothic tale.
He trails off, embarrassed perhaps
by such heartfelt complaint,
only to start up again like a distant, hooting train.

He must be hungry.
Or lonely.
The rope with which he is tethered rubs the sore spot on his neck.

There is a puppy I had dreamed of taking home in a small crate on
    a plane.
She arrived, somehow, at the beach with one *taverna*
where she eats fishheads and leftover rice
and smiles at people who walk down from the olive grove.
If she survives, she will be chained up
with two other hounds who bark and scratch in the sun.

But in spite of desire (which is not the same as a small crate)
I will not now take her home. From time to time
I will explain how getting home had become a problem,

how I had to think about lives more important than hers.
From time to time I will squat down in the dust
pretending to eat fish heads.

TELL THE WORLD THIS COOK WAS

| GOOD | BAD | SO-SO |

Against a neon sky
two shimmering towers
fade in and out
Look closely through cloud
he smuggled to the top
He shot the arrow,
friends caught the fishing line
hauled across cable,
Against a timeless sky
from New York '74
Swooping in the wind
with his balancing pole,
glides into space.
but by halfway across
and swings his right arm
(Far, far below,
a crowd converged
but none linger now,
the tightrope and the man
Against an eggshell sky
from tower to tower
His slippers stroke steel,
you can see him there still
sets the pole on his stomach,
Then, weight on the right foot,
to lift just a little
though rain has started
Against a neon sky,
sliding his feet
Philippe Petit

a stark silhouette:
faint and transparent
as they fly above the fog.
and you'll see the cable
of the silent South Tower.
its shaft a shooting star;
and fixed it to the roof,
anchored cavalettis.
that steel line stretches
off into the future.
the tiny wire walker
back lit by the dawn,
He grunts as he goes
he's humming, he kneels
in his signature salute.
small faces upturned,
and cop cars wailed —
the night sky holds only
treading like a torero.)
seven times he sashays
twirling midway.
his eyes on the far side —
as he slowly lies down,
spine flat on cable.
he waits for the wire
and stands up laughing
to spatter his skin.
night after night,
through the startled stars,
flies with the phantom twins.

the quizzical barred owl soars above the creek
which is swollen with sudden spring storms
and a man decides to go to war.

Actually, the decision was made long ago —
you could see it glinting in the man's eye
like that secret longing for a cold, amber whiskey

that betrays itself in overly measured words
or the military posture of the drunk
inspecting the troops in his dark overcoat.

Last year that owl, a fluffy youngster,
fell onto the highway where he walked unsteadily
on pencil legs back and forth across the center stripe.

The woman who found him placed him in the cradle
of her old hemlock and fed him live rats
until one day he took off. For months, though,

his coffee-and-cream striped and spotted form
would slip out of the rainforest at her call:
hoo hoo hoo! hoo hoo hoo!

Today is St. Patrick's Day. The trunks of alders
sprout skins of luminous moss while children
flaunt their green in the playground —

except for the one who has forgotten
and is pinched hard until she cries out:
Leave me alone! Leave me alone!

At the same time in this one world,
salt winds pleat the skin of Pacific dunes
and a shadow glides across Middle Eastern sand

where a woman in a doorway shades her eyes.
Her son's small feet are ashy.
His sandals have lost all trace of color.

GREAT TREE FALLING

First it totters just a bit
off balance — a little drunk
you might think, as you look
at its lacy crown against winter sky,
the smallest branches shuddering
as if they already sensed
the plunge that is about to begin
and how that plunge
will swing them in a wide arc:
sixty feet, seventy feet,
shearing off one whole side
of smaller trees on the way down.

Like a diver on a high board,
arms raised, breath gulped,
those twigs tease you,
change their minds and
hold on to the sky. The logger
sighs, yanks the cord of his chainsaw
and slips the soft blade into the notch,
cutting deeper into the heart.
Now, surely — fatally wounded
and sagging on the one leg
that has always reached for the earth's core —
now, surely, it will concede....

A crack like breaking bone,
a tremor, and the great trunk
tilts. Branches begin
to blunder through forest:
flung outwards

through maple and fir,
they rip the lichen
from hemlocks, snatch at
spars, tear whole limbs from
unsuspecting spruce and hurl
the debris away into the tangle
of salmonberries and slash.

Then it slows, hangs suspended: forty-five degrees;
thirty degrees: part of heaven
soon to become earth, but for now
you hold your breath, remembering how
yesterday you tied the pink ribbon
round its hips and marked it for this moment —
how you reached around its old torso,
your cheek pressed into wet bark,
feeling for a moment that hopeless love
for what you, yourself, condemned —
love, if you can call it that,
which changes nothing.

I cannot name the one with the scimitar beak and the mohawk
    who spends all day drilling holes in tree trunks.
I cannot name the enormous one with the white stocking cap
    on his head, hounded by glory and flags, poor devil.
I cannot name the thumblet with wings that whirr
    like the new kind of dentist's drill — Rupert or Rufus
    come to mind when I watch her at the scarlet feeder
    but I cannot be sure: the flash of her arrival
    too swift for color, is what matters in the long run.
I cannot name the one who hoots
    the one who dives from treetops
    the one who stands on chopstick legs
    waiting for sushi.
I cannot even name the caged one who calls himself "pretty"
    and mocks the world with his nasal chant
    nor the big white one on the beach who stabs
    the rotten flesh of his dead brother.
    Then there are those with the red vests or speckled chests:
I cannot name them either (or perhaps I simply will not).
    Unnamed, brownish ones doze on telephone poles
    hunched and grumpy as old men
    while the black-jacketed strut in the road
    rolling like sailors and holding up traffic.
I cannot name the tiny chirper who follows me along the creek
    moving so fast that I see nothing of bird, nothing
    of shape or weight or color or sex, nothing
    to look up in a book if I had a book or wanted a book.
I cannot even hazard a guess:
    She might be the spirit of my dead horse.
    She might be nobody.

♘ FIBONACCI

His numbers, *one one two, three five eight*—
each the sum of the two before,
appear like a rabbit from a hat

in the spiral of nautilus, the head
of each bowed sunflower—
even the two that sway in my front yard,

their papery stalks beginning to bend
from the work of holding up crestfallen heads.
And speaking of rabbits (which I was),

Fibonacci has a hand in the way they breed,
generations hopping to his golden rule—
the rule whose shadow lingers, a palimpsest

in the horn of mountain goat, parrot's beak,
the inevitable and precise curl
of an elephant's trunk. What symmetry!

Thirteen, twenty-one, thirty-four.
We could feel it in our bones if we tried:
human head to navel, navel to toes

or, traveling upward, belly button to the kissable
hollow of the throat and from there straight
to the highest point where as children

we balanced the ruler and made our mark:
three foot six, nineteen fifty-one never noticing
how our limbs reflect his math, never knowing

ourselves related by proportion to the shell
we would one day scoop up at the tide line
smiling at its oddly familiar grace.

NOTES

Page 59

"Passages" is a sequence of poems written as part of a collaboration with sculptor Nancy Azara for the wood-carved book of the same title.

Page 73

The words in italics in "Suicide Pact" are taken from *The Diary of Virginia Woolf, Volume Five, 1936-1941*, entries for May 20, May 30, and June 10, 1940.

Page 74

The words in italics in "Before I Am Born" are taken from *The Diary of Virginia Woolf, Volume Five, 1936-1941*, entry for September 15, 1940.

ABOUT THE AUTHOR

JUDITH BARRINGTON IS AN Anglo-American poet and memoirist. Her most recent book, *Lifesaving: A Memoir* was the winner of the Lambda Book Award and a finalist for the PEN/Martha Albrand Award for the Art of the Memoir and the Oregon Book Award. She is the author of two volumes of poetry, *Trying to Be an Honest Woman* and *History and Geography*, and *Writing the Memoir: From Truth to Art*.

Barrington's work has been has been published in numerous literary journals and in many anthologies, including *The Daily Telegraph Arvon International Poetry Competition Anthology 2000* and *The Bridport Prize 2003*.

With her partner, Ruth Gundle, she received the Stewart H. Holbrook Award from Oregon Literary Arts for outstanding service to Oregon's literary community. The Oregon Chapter of the American Civil Liberties Union honored her with their Freedom of Expression Award. She teaches at conferences and workshops across the U.S. as well as in Britain, and is one of the founders of Soapstone Inc., a writing retreat for women. She lives in Portland, Oregon.